...ME TO
PASSPORT TO READING
A beginning reader's ticket to a brand-new world!

Every book in this program is designed to build read-along and read-alone skills, level by level, through engaging and enriching stories. As the reader turns each page, he or she will become more confident with new vocabulary, sight words, and comprehension.

These PASSPORT TO READING levels will help you choose the perfect book for every reader.

READING TOGETHER
Read short words in simple sentence structures together to begin a reader's journey.

READING OUT LOUD
Encourage developing readers to sound out words in more complex stories with simple vocabulary.

READING INDEPENDENTLY
Newly independent readers gain confidence reading more complex sentences with higher word counts.

READY TO READ MORE
Readers prepare for chapter books with fewer illustrations and longer paragraphs.

This book features sight words from the educator-supported Dolch Sight Words List. This encourages the reader to recognize commonly used vocabulary words, increasing reading speed and fluency.

For more information, please visit passp... ...eadingbooks.com

Enjoy the jou...

D0376726

Little, Brown and Company

Hachette Book Group
1290 Avenue of the Americas, New York, NY 10104
Visit us at lb-kids.com

Little, Brown and Company is a division of Hachette Book Group, Inc.
The Little, Brown name and logo are trademarks of Hachette Book Group, Inc.

The publisher is not responsible for websites (or their content)
that are not owned by the publisher.

First Edition: May 2017

Library of Congress Control Number 2016953763

ISBNs: 978-0-316-54812-0 (paperback), 978-0-316-54810-6 (ebook),
978-0-316-55359-9 (ebook), 978-0-316-55361-2 (ebook)

10 9 8 7 6 5 4 3 2 1

CW

Printed in the United States of America

Passport to Reading titles are leveled by independent reviewers applying the
standards developed by Irene Fountas and Gay Su Pinnell in *Matching Books to
Readers: Using Leveled Books in Guided Reading*, Heinemann, 1999.

TEEN TITANS GO!

RAINY DAY HEROES

Adapted by Magnolia Belle

Based on the episode "I'm the Sauce"
written by H. Caldwell Tanner

L B

LITTLE, BROWN AND COMPANY
New York   Boston

Attention, Teen Titans fans!
Look for these words when you read
this book. Can you spot them all?

reading

cabin

volcano

rainbow

Beast Boy, Raven, Cyborg, and Starfire are all reading books on a sunny afternoon.

Robin bursts in through the door.
He shouts, "Titans!
Why are you inside when it is
such a beautiful day outside?"

The Titans want to keep reading.
Robin throws them outside so they have to play.

Robin tries to work on his tan.
But the sky fills with clouds.
It starts to rain.

Robin is sad.
He sends the Titans
back inside.

"Now may we go back to reading?" Starfire asks.

Robin replies, "No! Do you not know where rain comes from, Titans?"

Raven raises her hand. She answers, "When water vapor rises—"

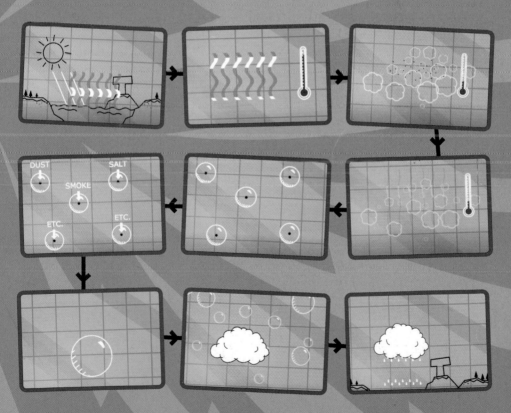

Robin interrupts her.
He says, "That is crazy, Raven!"

"Rain comes from clouds.
When clouds get sad, they cry.
Rain is cloud tears."

The Titans gasp.

They agree to cheer up the sad clouds!

Robin is excited.
He shows them a crazy dance
he calls the Spaghetti Dance.

He says the clouds will
be happy if they all do
the Spaghetti Dance.

The other Titans are shocked.

They will not do
the Spaghetti Dance.
It is too silly!

The Titans walk away from Robin. He will give them chocolate milk if they do other rainy-day activities.

The Titans love chocolate milk! They agree to help.

Beast Boy and Cyborg use Popsicle sticks to build a log cabin.

Raven makes a baking-soda volcano. It is a little too powerful.

Robin and Beast Boy play guessing games.

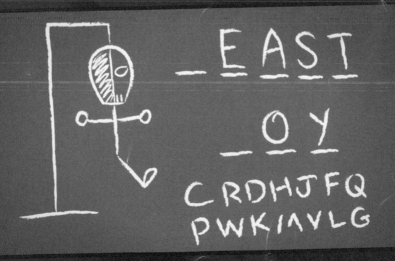

Then the Teen Titans try a game of hide-and-seek.

None of these fun games make
the clouds happy.
The clouds are still crying.
Robin begs the Titans to do
the Spaghetti Dance.
They will not.

"There is only one other option."
Robin says, "We have to play
Heads Up–Seven Up!"

Robin invites all the villains in the city to Titan Tower.

Robin tells them about the sad clouds.
He asks them to play Heads Up–Seven Up.

Robin offers them chocolate milk, and they all agree to play.

The Teen Titans and their villains play the most epic game of Heads Up–Seven Up ever.

The game works perfectly.
The clouds are happy again!

The Teen Titans
are a little sad now.

They miss the rain.
They want to do more
rainy-day activities.

The Teen Titans upset
the last cloud by calling
it names.

The cloud gets angry!
It becomes a terrible storm
cloud and attacks the Titans.

Robin says the Titans have to do the Spaghetti Dance to save the day!

The Teen Titans love the silly dance.

The cloud loves the silly dance, too.
The cloud laughs and bursts into
a beautiful rainbow!

The end.